Queer Windows

ISBN: 978-1-7364010-0-2 (paperback)
978-1-7364010-2-6 (BNP paperback)
978-1-7364010-1-9 (e-book)
First Edition 2022

Printed in the United States of America

Fox Fern Books, LLC

www.foxfernbooks.com

www.cayfletcher.com

Queer Windows

Volume 1 Spring

Cay Fletcher

 Fox Fern Books, LLC

For my wife and those

that dream of escaping to other worlds.

ALSO BY
CAY FLETCHER

ADULT FANTASY

The Kingdom Asleep in Thorns

TTRPG JOURNALS

The Chronicle Diary

The Ultimate Chronicle Diary

The Storyteller's Chronicle Diary

CONTENTS

AUTHOR'S NOTE

Some of the stories included in this volume have content warnings. They are listed for each story below.

THE WIZARD'S GARDEN

None.

ROSEMARY FOR REMEMBRANCE

Mentions of homophobia.

KINGDOM FALL

Mentions of assault, war, death/murder. Self-harm.

LADY OF SPRING

Mentions of parental death.

THE Wizard's Garden

Cay Fletcher

THE WIZARD'S GARDEN

SIL & ANDERS

STANDING IN FRONT OF THE old stone shop, Sil sucked in a chestfull of the crisp morning air. He had already inspected the old wooden sign hanging above the door and made certain that the flower boxes hanging below the windows looked perfect.

The opening of the garden shop was a signal that spring was close at hand.

Beren, the easy-going owner, had taken over the shop, with its huge glass greenhouse, from her parents almost a decade ago and Sil had spent the last several years learning everything he could about the unique selection of plants they sold. He had been promoted to the senior clerk at the end of last season. Though, promoted might be a strong term, as the previous senior clerk had retired after a nasty tangle with an octopus bramble bush. But all the same, Sil was determined to prove that he was a valuable asset to the shop.

All the usual herbs were out in pots, trimmed to be perfectly appealing to anyone looking to add a little spice to their potions. The flowers were slowly waking up, petals stretching out as the early morning sun rose higher in the sky, light streaming in through the greenhouse glass. Sil carefully inspected each pot, pressing a finger into the cool soil and watering the ones that felt dry. Everything needed to go perfectly. A good opening day would show Beren that he had everything under control.

With the watering done, Sil straightened his apron and looked over the tables of plants. He leaned over a display of carnivorous plants and put on his bossiest tone, "Today is very important. I don't think any of you want to ruin it, so be on your best behavior."

Magda, donning a sweatshirt with her university's pixie mascot on the front, sipped loudly at her iced coffee, "Are you going to berate them if they're bad?"

Sil pushed his glasses up the bridge of his nose, "What good would that do?"

With a shrug, Magda replied, "You're the 'expert'. You tell me."

"I don't have time to go over the theories for keeping plants happy and harmonious in a shop setting," Sil said dismissively and walked over to the snapdragons. A part of him preened at the title of 'expert', even if it was meant as a jab. Most of the brightly colored blooms were still snoozing, but a few were awake and nuzzling each other. The bell that signaled the door opening rang brightly, and he heard Magda mumble a greeting.

"You lot, no biting anyone today," Sil softly instructed the sleepy flowers.

He could feel someone standing behind him. They leaned over and let the snapdragons nip at their fingers, "You know, if you give them a little honey, they listen better."

The man's deep voice was warmly familiar. Standing stiff as a board, Sil slipped out of the man's way, his optimistic mood suddenly darkened by the man's appearance, "We can't spoil them in a shop setting. They might turn on a new owner if they don't keep up with the care that we provided. You of all people should know that, Anders."

Smiling at the snapdragons, Anders shook his head, "Honey wouldn't spoil you, would it?"

They nipped more at his fingers and rustled together in agreement.

"Is there something I can help you with, sir?" Sil snapped at the wizard. Somehow the man always looked disheveled, his velvet cloak tattered and worn, the seams of his sleeves fraying and stained with ink.

"Sir? No need to be so formal, Sil. I've been shopping here for years," he said as he continued to tickle the snapdragons. "But I suppose you might be able to assist me with finding something."

Bristling, Sil readied himself for another of Anders' outrageous requests. He was in the shop almost every week buying plant after plant. Surely the wizard had an entire graveyard full of the poor things. Sil could picture the stacks of pots, the soil dried out and hydrophobic, the withered remains of once lush, green foliage shivering in the breeze. Beren wouldn't have kept selling to him if she knew that the wizard was in the business of killing plants, right? It was a truly horrid image, and he shook his head to banish it from his thoughts.

He certainly hadn't anticipated Anders being their first customer of the season, and he felt it would cast a bad omen over his new position. At least the man hadn't gone to Magda for help, she hardly knew the difference between the uses of lemon balm and lavender and she was likely to let him buy whatever he wanted.

"What is it you're looking for, Mr. Anders?"

Sil asked him.

"Just Anders is okay, Sil. Though I wish you'd tell me your full name," the wizard replied with a chuckle. "Sil seems so… silly."

Sil was certain that anyone nearby could sense his disdain at the pun, "And let you cast all kinds of spells on me? No. I think not."

"Is it Sylvestre?" There was a knowing twinkle in Anders' eyes.

"It's not short for anything," Sil replied firmly.

"I'll figure it out eventually," he stroked his chin for a moment before pulling a small glass bottle out of a hidden pocket in his cloak. Holding it up to the light, Sil could see tiny specks of what looked like dirt flitting around, "My garden has recently been infested with dust mites. I was hoping you might have something to repel them."

Sil's eyes widened a bit, "And you brought them here?"

"They're quite contained, don't worry." Anders shook the bottle gently, "Oh, and I need something new for the front herb garden. I have all the usual things, but I'm rather bored with it."

"Salt and vinegar is the best thing to get rid of dust mites," Sil said, bristling at the thought that anyone could be bored with their garden. Plants were living things, even if they weren't as 'interesting' as pets. "We have spray bottles over with the supplies."

"I don't want to kill them, just encourage them to move along."

Sil blinked at the wizard for a moment, "Are you intent upon making up headstones for your poor plants then?"

The wizard shrugged, "They have their place, just as anyone does. I just don't want them dusting every plant I'm using for research. I've tried planting ivy, I heard they like that, but they haven't taken to it."

"My gram used to leave out candy near where she was okay with them living," Magda said in a bored tone, "Though. I'm pretty sure the gnomes ate most of it. They got rather fat not long after."

Anders chuckled, "I don't have gnomes yet. I'm working on cultivating some mushrooms for them first."

"Why would you want to encourage gnomes to live in your garden? They attract all sorts of pests," Sil said, horrified. The situation was far worse than he could have imagined. Was Anders wrangling every pest and animal to feast on the poor plants he purchased every week like an open buffet?

"Pests? Y'know, humans are probably pests

to them. Always chasing them out of their homes, or blocking off their usual food. I think we should try to live more harmoniously with them," Anders explained.

"Why don't we come back to the dust mites?" Sil suggested, starting to feel exasperated. "What types of herbs were you looking for?"

"I thought fire curry might be fun," Anders said, leaning over the display of walking succulents and tickling one. The succulent curled up its plump leaves much like an anemone.

"We don't keep fire curry in the shop. It's only available on special order, as it's too dangerous," he could just imagine the scorched remains of a herb bed that was unprepared to be living next to something so volatile.

"Drat, I was really hoping for some. Spicy food makes the gray days all the better, and it's been so rainy and dull lately. I don't think I have the space for creeping oregano. Maybe some catnip? I might be able to enlist the neighborhood cats into helping with the dust mites."

Crossing his arms, Sil said, "The cats will probably chase away your other pests. If they're good mousers at least. We can order the fire curry for you to pick up. If you have an appropriate planting space for it."

"Hrm, I much prefer the cats that lie in

sunspots all day. For the fire curry though, can you deliver it?" Anders asked.

"That's not usually—"

Sil felt a hand on his shoulder and turned to find his boss smiling gently, curly moss dangling from her own dark curls. "Of course we can, Anders. You've always been one of our best customers, and I think Sil would enjoy visiting your garden."

"Thank you, Beren, I think I'll see what else you have that's new and then make that order," Anders said with a grin. "By the way, your moss is lovely."

Beren gently stroked the moss cascading down her curls, "I thought it would be a nice change from the mushrooms. They're enjoying their new log out back."

"I'm sure they are. I'll be sure to say goodbye before I'm finished shopping," Anders said as he wandered off.

"He's always so sweet. He once helped me save a whole crop of angry dandelions from being mowed over in a park."

"I guess a wizard would be perfect for that sort of thing," Sil grumbled, "But we don't deliver. And I don't think we should be selling him fire curry. He's not on the registry of approved owners and he's always buying new plants. Do we really know he's properly taking care of them? His garden could be a graveyard for everything we've let him buy, for all we know."

Smiling, Beren started tickling the leaves of a new fennec fern, "If you're that concerned about the state of his plants, then you should make the delivery. Then you can see for yourself."

"Well yes," he said with a sigh, glancing over at the wizard who was now bent over examining a pallet of herbs rather intently. Maybe he could rescue a few tormented plants.

Sil slid off his bicycle and leaned it against the fence once he reached the address scribbled down on the order pad. A neglected mailbox stood atop a post being choked by ivy, but there was no sign of a house or even a hut beyond the old wooden gate. Double-checking the number on the pad and the one on the mailbox they seemed to match. If the wizard had somehow gotten his address wrong, Sil wouldn't be surprised. Beren had made it sound like the wizard had an extensive garden, but all Sil could see was a poorly tended lawn and some scrappy shrubs along the fence line.

Stepping over the worst of the mud

puddles in the road, he tried to see if maybe there was another house hidden behind the collection of scraggly oak trees, but the countryside was only broken up by wandering lines of fencing and the occasional hedge.

"Well this is perfect," Sil said to himself.

Going back to the gate, he noticed a small sign which had flipped over in the wind.

"'State your name for deliveries?'" Sil read out loud, glancing at the empty lot beyond the fence. He desperately hoped this wasn't some kind of joke.

"Sil, here with your fire curry plant, Mr. Anders," nothing seemed to happen as he stood there on the quiet, empty lane. The longer he stood there, the dumber he felt. Clearly, this was Anders somehow getting back at him for the years of underhanded comments and he was going to have to bike all the way back to the shop with a chilly, grumpy, fire curry plant.

"Oh, you're early," Anders' voice came from down the lane. Sil jumped, catching himself against the gate as he turned to see Anders striding down the lane without a care in the world. The wizard was attempting to wrestle something back under his cape.

"Where did you come from?"

"I was visiting my neighbor," Anders said,

grinning at him as if appearing from thin air was a normal thing.

"So this is the right address?"

"Of course!" Anders said, opening the gate before stopping abruptly, "Oh dear, the house is still playing hide and seek. This may be a problem."

"I would think so. I'll just get the fire curry out and be on my way, Mr. Anders," Sil said. The last thing he wanted was to be involved in whatever wizarding problems Anders was currently having. That was how someone ended up a wizard's apprentice. Or worse, friend.

"No, no, at least have some tea for your trouble. Just give me a moment to find the house," as Anders wandered off the stone path and into the front garden a tiny, fuzzy, black, head popped up out of his collar. Little tendrils of smoke twisted around its whiskers as the pipe dragon's golden eyes fixated on Sil.

"It's really alright, no need to go out of your way-" Sil insisted, hurriedly pulling on the oven mitts and fireproof apron he'd brought with him. The faster he could hand over the fire curry the better as all hopes of rescuing any suffering plants vanished from his thoughts.

"Ah, found it!" Anders declared, either ignoring Sil's protests or not hearing him. He held up a brick and waved it for Sil to see.

"Oooookay, time to get the hell out of here," Sil muttered to himself, unzipping the heat-proof grocery bag that was strapped into the basket on the front of his bicycle. "Don't burn me. I'm just giving you over to a crazy wizard. You'll be fine. He has a pipe dragon, so I'm sure that will go over well."

He could feel something looming over him and jumped again, nearly dropping the fire curry, as he turned to find Anders standing next to him, "You like talking to them, don't you?"

"I um…" Sil hoped that the wizard hadn't heard him calling him crazy.

The pipe dragon wrapped its narrow, snake-like body around Anders' neck so it could watch Sil more closely. He was impressed that Anders had a pipe dragon, given how they'd nearly disappeared after being treated as common pests.

"Don't worry, they can hear you at least. And more people talk to 'inanimate' objects than you think. It's not that strange," Anders assured him. Chirping, the pipe dragon tried coiling down Anders' arm, "Ah, ah, ah, leave the nice garden clerk alone. He doesn't need you biting him."

"I'm sure he doesn't bite too hard," Sil said.

Anders snorted, "Maybe not, but he tends to get attached to strangers."

"I didn't think pipe dragons were still around."

"They're pretty rare. I rescued this guy from a drainpipe a few years ago. I'm hoping to start up a new colony of them here."

"That would be nice. I know a lot of gardeners like them around to help keep mites and rodents out of their gardens."

Anders rubbed the little dragon's head, "Hear that, you should be helping me with the dust mites."

It chirped innocently before retreating under Anders collar, "I'm afraid he's no good at mite hunting. I've got flower mites now too."

Sil frowned, "They shouldn't be out this time of year. It's still too chilly."

"True, but they're around all the same. Speaking of, let's get that fire curry settled before it catches its death," Anders said, heading back towards the gate.

Carefully holding the fire curry out in front of him, Sil gaped at the moss-covered, thatched cottage sitting where previously there had been an empty lot. Smoke filtered from the chimney, and a large stone bed of herbs lay under the front windows. Lush greenery surrounded the cottage, filling the yard to the point of bursting.

"Are you alright?" Anders asked him, concern in his tone.

Nodding slowly, Sil looked back and

forth between the neighboring lots and the newly appeared cottage. A robin landed on the edge of the roof and sang happily as if the house had in fact been there the whole time. It was a cute little house, and it fit with Anders personality. Though, there was no possibility that all of the tender, tropical and rare plants that Sil had witnessed Anders purchase over the years could fit inside it. Unless it was bigger on the inside.

"Sil?" Anders was peering at him, hand outstretched as if he was ready to shake Sil's shoulder.

Coming back to his senses, Sil cleared his throat, "Where do you want it?"

Anders held open the gate for Sil and pointed towards the herb bed, "I think out front might be best."

"It might enjoy a warmer spot. This bed is east facing."

"Hrm, well the south side of the garden is pretty full. And the herb bed is warmed."

"The soil is warmed?"

"Yes, I have ceramic pipes with warm water running through them throughout the bed. No magic required. It's a bit of an experiment."

He wasn't familiar with the technique, but it could work in theory, even if it was unconventional. Sil set the fire curry on the stone edge of the bed and pulled off one of the oven mitts so he could rest his hand on the soil. It was warmer than he would have expected, almost like the sun had been shining on it all day, "I guess that might be okay. Though really you should have a soil thermometer to ensure the bed is keeping the right temperature. If you mulched this bed it would help keep that heat in better."

Anders nodded, "I keep forgetting to do that. Maybe I could pay you for some yard work? If you're interested I mean."

"You'd pay me to do yard work?" Sil asked skeptically, moving the fire curry to a spot in the bed where it might do well and was far enough from the other plants. He could always use the extra money. But was working for Anders worth it?

"Yes, Beren clearly trusts you. And you seem to care a lot about plants. It would give me more time for research," Anders said as he wandered around the corner of the house towards the backyard.

Sil followed after him, surprised by the sheer amount of rare and unusual plant life all seemingly coexisting in such a temperate area. Half of the plants, large brightly colored flowers, towering palms, and other tender stemmed plants thrived in tropical or arid climates which were very different from the cool, dreary, gray days of early spring in their area. The path along the side of the house even seemed pleasantly warm compared to the front, which couldn't all be due to the sun.

"How do you have so many plants out of season?" he asked, pushing his glasses up his nose to examine a dragon orchid growing from the trunk of a palm. It was thriving against all odds. Maybe Anders wasn't just letting his plants die. The cost of replacing them would be enormous given the selection.

"A micro-climate spell. Come, I want to show you where the mites have been troublesome," Anders said, waving him along the moss-covered path.

"Leave it to a wizard to figure out that kind of spell I guess," Sil muttered to himself, a bit jealous. He'd never be able to keep even a fraction of what was in Anders' garden in his tiny apartment. Anders' freedom to buy and keep whatever he liked had always upset Sil, limited by both budget and space.

As he entered the back garden, Sil stopped and stared at what appeared to be a forest of every plant he'd ever seen or heard of. Sections were marked off by woven fences and paths winding around and disappearing behind taller, bushier vegetation. He wanted to spend the hours it would take to wander Anders' backyard with his notebook, scribbling down all the varieties he wanted to look up.

"How? All this wasn't here before."

Anders grinned, "The garden is connected to the house, so if I move, the garden doesn't get left behind to fall into disrepair. It's a rather simple translocation spell actually."

He knelt down and motioned along with one of the paths which curved off to the left. As Sil followed it with his eyes, he realized that the connecting paths helped form a large magical inscription, "The spell is built into the garden?"

Sil quickly let it sink in that someone that had spent the time to magically connect their garden to their house so it wouldn't be left behind, was unlikely to be a bad plant-parent on purpose. In fact, Anders had always asked questions about the plants before he ended up purchasing them. It left him feeling uncomfortable about judging the man so harshly based on their limited interactions at the shop.

"Yes, clever, don't you think?" Anders asked enthusiastically.

"I would think so. But I don't know that much about magic."

"I could teach you some of the basic things."

"Like the micro-climate spell?" Sil asked hopefully.

"Probably. Though, it might benefit you to learn the fundamentals first. A watering spell might be a good start," Anders started before trailing off into thought.

"I can start next week," he found himself saying before he could stop himself.

"Are you sure?"

"So long as you're fine with me working around my usual shifts at the shop."

"I don't see why that would be a problem. I'm usually around doing one thing or another."

Sil held out his hand to shake, "Great, I'll see you next week then."

"Not so worried about entering a contract with a wizard now, are you?" Anders asked as he took Sil's hand in agreement.

"You're paying me. If anything, you should be more concerned about what my rate is," Sil said smugly, though Anders' comment did start his mind spinning into an infinite number of possibilities.

Anders shook his head with a smile, "True. Maybe I should have negotiated that first."

"You've agreed, so you'll just have to suffer knowing you didn't."

"Are you certain you're not a wizard looking to bespell someone?"

Sil shrugged, "We haven't had a wizard in the family before."

Turning Sil's hand over in his own, Anders examined the lines on Sil's palm, "If you say so. There's never a bad time to add a witch or wizard to the family."

Sil shivered as Anders' finger traced a line from his palm up to his wrist. What could Anders tell from his hand that he couldn't tell with just looking at him? He doubted he would be any good at whatever magic Anders tried to teach him anyway. His talents lay strictly with raising plants.

Pulling his hand away, Sil cleared his throat and straightened his glasses, "Well, we have an agreement. So I'll see you next week."

"Yes. Be sure to bring a hat, the weather is supposed to be sunny and I wouldn't want you to get sunburnt."

Sil rolled his eyes as he followed the path back around the cottage and down to the gate. He looked up at the cottage and the garden before stuffing his oven mitts and apron into the basket and turning down the muddy road. He wished he had anything close to the garden that Anders had. Instead, he had a lonely shelf over his kitchen sink stuffed with an array of tiny pots of herbs and a pothos his mother had given him to nurse back to health. It was ninety-five percent function, and he had nowhere to expand in his tiny flat.

Anders' garden was quickly becoming Sil's favorite place, even if Anders' promise to teach him a few spells wasn't going well. After not even a week, he had already managed to chase the dust mites from the lily patch back to a specially prepared fern patch at the rear of the garden. Though he suspected that without a more permanent solution they would likely move back. He'd also discovered a family of gnomes living under an old willow and convinced them that stealing the red caps for haberdashery purposes wouldn't be needed if Anders provided some tiny wool caps. Anders had been a bit miffed, but Sil insisted that leaving the mushrooms alone would be better for the garden's overall ecosystem.

The pipe dragon had decided that his apron pocket was the perfect nap spot and would often scurry out of a bush to slip into it. Anders had assured him that it was good luck to keep a sleeping dragon on you and that the risk of burns were minimal.

One of the many strange things though, was Anders' insistence that he always leave before dark. The wizard never gave an explanation, and while Sil was curious, he didn't want to risk upsetting Anders and losing the opportunity to work in the garden.

"You've been here every day for the last week. Shouldn't you take a day off?" Anders asked him as he handed over a warm cup of tea.

Sil shrugged and sipped at the tea absently with one hand and pruned an unruly rhododendron that was overgrowing one of the paths with the other. "I'd just be at home. Reading. Or taking care of my own plants."

"Oh, you shouldn't neglect them," Anders said worriedly.

"They're fine. They don't need nearly as much attention as your garden does," namely due to their inferior number in comparison.

Anders sighed and leaned his head back, "Okay, just don't exhaust yourself. Beren wouldn't forgive me if I wore out her favorite employee."

"Favorite?" Sil asked, a bit surprised.

"Of course. Why else would she promote you? No offense, but you're a little young to be the lead clerk. And grumpy."

"I'm not that young. I live by myself, thank you," he couldn't refute the grumpy comment. Anders didn't seem to mind his disposition much.

"You're twenty."

Sil rounded on Anders, "Twenty-one! And you're not much older than me. And besides, you're a wizard! Who says you should have that much power and responsibility?"

Setting aside his tea, Anders leaned in towards Sil, "I've been training since I was a child."

"And I've been raising plants since I was a child."

"What was your first rare plant then?" Anders asked him, challenging him.

"Tuft tails. They only grow along a single river bank and only flower for about a week. I had one when I was ten and kept it alive in my bedroom window."

"Tuft tails?"

"Commonly known as feather duster plants," Sil explained smugly.

"Ahhhhh, alright, not bad."

"Not bad?" any normal plant enthusiast would be impressed, but of course, Anders was far from normal.

"It's not as if you were raising fire curry at age ten."

"That's because fire curry shouldn't be raised by a child!" Sil said, outraged.

Anders chuckled, "You're very talented Sil."

"Don't patronize me."

"I'm not patronizing you. You are talented."

"Then why can't I make that stupid watering spell work?"

"You've only been practicing it for a week. It's expected that you wouldn't be able to make it work yet."

"How long did it take you?" Sil asked him.

"A couple…days."

"See?"

"That's only because I already knew other spells. It goes quicker once you know a bit more. You'll get the hang of it."

Sil snipped off the last few rhododendron branches that were intruding on the walkway, "I'm going to go mulch the front herb bed. Unless you need to torment me with something else."

Anders smiled, "I'm not tormenting you."

"Uh-huh."

"You agreed to work for me, might I remind you."

"For the plants."

"You wound me, Silvan," Anders replied dramatically.

"It's not Silvan. Just Sil," he grumbled, careful not to drop the sheers on the pipe dragon's head in his apron pocket in his annoyance.

"Okay, okay. I'll be back here looking over the spider plants. They seem out of sorts."

Taking his tea, Sil went around to the front of the house where the herb bed was. There were all the usual suspects, rosemary, oregano, six types of basil, marjoram, thyme, and of course the new fire curry among numerous other plants Sil wasn't familiar with. Some spearmint was taking over the back corner of the raised planting bed, threatening to encroach on the rest of the plants. Everything needed a trim, the weeds desperately needed to be pulled and the mulch would help keep everything neat.

He set aside his tea and started trimming back the rosemary, making sure to toss them into a bowl for Anders to use later. With all of Anders' spells, Sil was surprised that he hadn't cast one to prune all the plants at the correct times. Though it did give him something to do. And a chance to play in Anders' garden. The pipe dragon slithered out of his apron pocket and coiled around his neck, its whiskers tickling his jaw.

"Hey, stop that!" Sil tried to rearrange the pipe dragon, "Settle down or you have to go back into the apron."

Chirping at him, the pipe dragon finally settled on his shoulder.

Sighing, Sil started on the oregano, "Why is he so impossible?"

The pipe dragon trilled almost in understanding.

"And why can't I get this damn spell to work?" Sil asked, setting down the sheers and mimicking the hand motions that Anders had shown him. A few tiny drops of water appeared between Sil's hands and the pipe dragon raised its head and chirped happily before the drops fizzled into steam.

"See? I'm useless."

The pipe dragon nuzzled his neck.

"It's fine. I'll always have plants."

Nipping at his neck the pipe dragon twirled its body around Sil's upper arm.

"And you. So long as you stop chewing on me," Sil told it, getting back to tidying up the herb bed. "Now, all of you, how is the fire curry fitting in? I don't see any scorch marks, so that's good. Though, mint, if you keep trying to choke out the other herbs, I'm going to take a trowel to you and move you to your own pot. So behave, won't you?"

He sighed when there was no response from the mint. There was never an expectation they would talk back, though some of the more magically inclined plants would respond in other ways. Sil was getting far too used to Anders talking back. Even in the week he'd been there, he was finding Anders' company enjoyable, and his life away from the garden incredibly lonely. That might have been the largest contributor to Sil being willing to ride his bike across town and out into the country lanes to Anders cottage.

As he finished pruning and put a layer of mulch on the soil, his mind began to wander and he stared at his reflection in the window that the herb bed stood under. He unconsciously pushed his glasses back up his nose and grumbled at the sight of leaves and twigs stuck in his hair. His parents always complained about his penchant to drag the outdoors inside. The window above the herb bed was home to a spider who had taken upon itself to weave a web that could only be rivaled by the best lacemakers. Spiders were always a good sign in a garden as they helped take care of flies and other pests. Though, a thought struck him, growing up, his tuft tail had always prevented the house spiders from making their webs in his bedroom window. If they tried, the tuft tails would sweep their fibrous flowers across the corners of the window, gently removing the webs, but not harming the spider.

Tuft tails might be the answer to Anders' dust mite problem. They were bound to make their way back to the lilies if left to their own devices. If not spread to any number of other plants. But a line of tuft tails around their current home in the ferns would gently prevent them from leaving the area. Anders might have to create a new micro-climate spell to keep them happy, but it was worth a try.

Running around to the backyard, the pipe dragon slipped under Sil's collar so it wouldn't lose its grip. Sil skidded to a stop in front of Anders and said, "I need tuft tails."

Anders stopped mid-spell and blinked up at him, "Right now?"

"To keep the dust mites contained."

The spark of realization dawned over Anders' face, "Of course! Why didn't I think of that?"

"Because you didn't raise one when you were ten."

Anders pulled Sil into a hug and spun him around, "And that's why I have you, Sirik."

"Still just Sil," Sil said, too surprised to push Anders away.

"I can probably have Beren order some."

"You'll need a micro-climate spell for them to do well," Sil said, finally escaping the hug.

"Right, you can give me the details on that. Tomorrow though. It's almost dark, so you should get going."

Sil hadn't even noticed how late it had gotten, "I still have things to put away. I don't mind it being a little dark."

Anders frowned, "It's not ready for you to see yet."

"What isn't ready?" maybe Anders had mentioned something and Sil had just turned him out.

"Your surprise."

Sil snorted, "Surprise? Why would you

have a surprise for me?”

Anders scratched the back of his neck sheepishly, “Because you’ve been such a big help.”

“I’ve been working for you for a week.”

“At Beren’s shop too though. You always have ideas for new varieties of plants, or how to help them grow healthier. You’ve worked there for almost five years, right?”

“Yes, but I help everyone there. It’s my job.”

“Even slightly crazy wizards.”

Sil felt his face grow hot, “I shouldn’t have called you crazy.”

Anders shrugged, “It’s okay. It happens a lot.”

“That doesn’t make it okay.”

“I guess not, but I’d rather have a friend than dwell on that,” he turned towards the garden and clapped his hands together twice. As if on command, every plant and bloom in the garden stood at attention, looking their best and brightest. A swarm of fireflies flew into the middle of the garden and began blinking, spelling out ‘Thank you Sil.’

“I wanted to give them more time to practice, but…”

“You did all this for me?” Sil asked, feeling tears starting to well up.

“Of course.”

Sil wiped at his eyes and wrapped his arms around Anders' neck, "You're not a crazy wizard. You're a silly one."

"So…does this mean we're friends?"

"Yes, so long as you don't have plans of making me an apprentice."

Anders started to laugh, "You're the one that wanted to learn magic! And somehow I think you already are."

"Oh yes, I can! And who says I am?"

"Don't worry about the label so much. What do you want to learn next?"

Sil nearly started a retort, but stopped himself, "As much as possible."

ROSEMARY
FOR
REMEMBRANCE

Cay Fletcher

ROSEMARY FOR REMEMBRANCE

VIV & THE STRANGER

VIVIAN SET DOWN HER bucket and trowel before kneeling in the least muddy spot in front of the herb patch. The rain had been a constant downpour so she had taken the first sun break as an opportunity to weed out the little section of the garden where she grew herbs. Her local murder of crows were also taking the break in the weather as a chance to root around for worms and other insects, cawing loudly to each other.

The misty dampness of spring was always one of Vivian's favorite times of the year to be out in the garden. Woody herbs like rosemary, which had been cut back in the fall, had bright green new growth, and bulbs had begun to poke up from the muddy soil. Her garden was nothing special, just room enough for herbs and some greens and flowers from packets of seeds she'd been saving from before the war. One day she dreamed of having terraced vegetable beds with a stone or brick path winding through rose bushes, and a secret nook to enjoy the morning. But she did what she could with the borrowed patch of land on the side of the house where she rented the bottom-floor apartment.

Skirts spread around her with little care for the dirt, she began to hum to herself as she gently pulled out the weeds around her precious plants. Growing things was like magic. She planted a seed where it would be warm and flourish, watered it, and tended to the earth around it, and then a tiny sprout emerged. That sprout would eventually become something useful, like lavender and chamomile blossoms for a relaxing tea, mint, and ginger for an upset stomach, and so much more.

Outside of her garden, the world seemed to be in a whirlwind. Wars were still being fought in the east, her young cousin had just shipped off to a post in Korea. Seemingly regular people were being charged with espionage. And everyone was teetering on the edge of their seats, waiting for the sound of air sirens to signal bombs or missiles. Yet life went on as if ignoring the precarious state of the world and its secrets. She retreated to her garden, away from the constant sound of her upstairs neighbor's radio, dreaming of the far-off places she'd only know between the pages of books.

Clouds shifted and unfurled as the wind began bringing in the next storm, but Vivian kept at her weeding, determined to finish before the rain came back. Inside, was the stack of papers that she had yet to grade, and the lesson plans she had meant to finish before falling asleep the night before. The garden was her refuge.

One of the crows hopped over to the stone which acted as an impromptu birdbath, a snail in its beak, and tilted its head curiously at Vivian. She'd yet to formally meet all the crows that lived in the tall fir trees that stood sentry over the little garden every morning, most of them were still wary of her presence in their usual breakfast spot.

"Good morning. It looks as if you've found your breakfast."

The crow dropped the snail into the water pooled in the bowl of the stone and began picking at it.

Smiling and sitting back on her heels, Vivian added, "I do appreciate you keeping the snails from eating my herbs. Maybe I can leave you some of the snails I find. Though I'd like to see the worms survive if you wouldn't mind."

Paying her no attention, the crow fished the snail from its shell and flew away again. "If you feed them, they'll start bringing you gifts," a tired-sounding voice informed her. The owner was casually dressed in an oversized sweater, jeans, short rubber boots with a knit cap covering their cropped hair. Vivian wasn't certain where they could be going looking like a poorly dressed fisherman. Maybe it was the fashion in the city now? As the clouds shifted again, the edges of the stranger blurred, like a watercolor painting. The visual anomaly was gone a moment later.

"I can't say I really need more trinkets, but I certainly wouldn't mind it," Vivian replied.

The stranger squatted down, inspecting the lemon thyme that looked a bit worse for wear, "What's this?"

When they met Vivian's eyes, she couldn't help but be entranced by the stranger's dark brown ones. Catching the light, they shone and almost glowed a golden color.

"Lemon thyme. This winter was a bit too cold for its liking."

"I'm sure it will come back. You seem to have a green thumb."

"Do you live nearby? I could give you some cuttings if you would like," Vivian offered.

Thinking for a moment as they rubbed a

sprig of the lemon thyme between their fingers, releasing its strong scent, they finally shook their head, "I really shouldn't. Taking things home isn't the best idea."

"Oh, can you not have plants?"

"That's not it. I have a garden back home. It can get a little complicated."

Vivian wasn't entirely certain she understood, but she didn't want to press, "Well, if you want to take some, you are welcome to. I could never use all of it."

"Maybe I'll take some of the rosemary, for remembrance."

"Doesn't Ophelia say that?"

The stranger smiled, "She does."

That smile hung between them as the breeze pulled Vivian's curls into her eyes. She tucked them behind her ear and realized that the stranger was still watching her intently, "Could I get you some tea? You could come in for a spell?"

"I'm really just passing through."

The watery edges of the stranger's clothes were becoming more blurred once more, as if they were slowly fading away, "I'm sure you'll have the garden of your dreams one day."

"What?" the comment made Vivian pause as if she'd missed a few sentences in their conversation.

"A bigger garden. With a path and a coffee nook, right?" The stranger's smile was so disarming, even as Vivian began to realize how dream-like the situation was. They couldn't be real.

"One day I want a bigger garden, yes."

With a nod the stranger held out their hand, "It was good meeting you Miss Vivian."

Vivian reached out to shake the stranger's hand, not sure if she'd given her name. But the screen door slamming in the wind behind her drew her gaze for a moment, and when she'd turned back, the stranger was gone. Blinking, Vivian stood and looked up and down the lane, even stepping around her precious herbs and leaning over the wrought iron fence. They couldn't possibly have disappeared, could they have? Pulling her cardigan tighter around herself as the wind rushed by again, she realized she was holding a sprig of rosemary she'd never picked.

Weeks had passed since Vivian's odd encounter with the stranger, and while she'd hoped to see them in town, there had been no sign of them. Instead, the strange meeting had been put to a page in her diary where her all musings could live alongside her most secret dreams. The stranger had been quite handsome, roguish even, given the tilt to their smile, and how their fringe fell into their eyes. She wished she would have asked their name, so she knew what to call them at the very least.

It was an unusually warm day for April and the bees were making short work of finding every new flower. Clipping some mint next to the gate and slipping it absently into the basket on her arm, along with the other herbs she'd been cutting, she noticed a bicycle leaning up against the posts. It looked brand new, with shiny blue paint and a white leather seat, no signs of rust or wear. Far too nice to belong to any of the kids that lived in the area. They loved racing through the puddles on the side roads so their bicycles were always coated in mud. Gently running her fingertips over the leather-wrapped handlebars, Vivian noticed that familiar but strange faded look clung to the edges of the bicycle.

"Oh, you found it," the stranger called out, appearing so suddenly behind Vivian that she stumbled backward. They caught Vivian easily in their arms, steadying her with a grin. "Sorry about that."

Vivian quickly put some distance between the two of them, smoothing out her gingham dress while sizing up the stranger out of the corner of her eye.

"Isn't it a bit warm for such a heavy jacket?" Vivian asked.

The stranger looked down at themselves and shrugged, "I thought the aviator would be more appropriate."

"Appropriate for what?"

"The time."

Frowning, Vivian felt the confusion knitting between her brows, "I didn't realize that pilots had a certain time of day they were appropriate."

"No, I meant..." the stranger chuckled, giving Vivian a sweet smile as they peered up at her. They scratched the back of their head as if sorting through how to answer.

"Meant what?"

"Never mind. I only have a little while before I have to be back."

Vivian allowed the change of subject, "Back where?"

"Home."

"And where is home?" Vivian asked, finding herself hoping that it might be close by.

The stranger chuckled again, "I don't think you'd believe me."

"You're already odd, try me."

"You know about fairy circles?"

Vivian stared at the stranger for a moment in confusion. She had asked, but she had expected that they were some sort of performer or maybe an eccentric carpet bagger, "I know of the concept from children's fairy tales."

"Well, imagine a fairy circle that could transport you somewhere else. Maybe some other time."

Vivian gave the stranger a disbelieving look, her finger starting to tap against her arm, "You're saying you came through a fairy circle like the Pevensies go through the wardrobe to Narnia."

Smiling warmly, the stranger nodded, "That's a much better analogy. I wasn't certain that you'd read it."

"I'm a school teacher, I try to keep up with the latest children's books."

"Well, I'm definitely not from Narnia."

"I wouldn't think so. You hardly look like you could hide a pair of fawn's legs in those trousers."

The stranger shrugged, "You never know. Appearances can be deceiving."

"Because people can't just walk through magical wardrobes or fairy circles to other worlds."

"Have you ever tried?" the stranger asked, more earnestly than Vivian expected.

"Well," Vivian sputtered. Hadn't most children imagined traveling to strange new worlds? Especially when the real one was dark and full of danger? Glancing away, Vivian nodded, "When I was younger I pretended to go on adventures in my grandmother's garden."

"What sorts of adventures?"

"Exploring the jungles of South America, or documenting the fairy life of the neighborhood," Vivian said shyly.

Leaning against the fence, the stranger pulled a small notebook from their pocket and scribbled a few notes in it, "You're more fascinating than I could have imagined, Miss Vivian."

A cloud moved over the sun and for a moment, the stranger almost appeared transparent, "Wait, I never gave you my name."

"Oh?" the stranger seemed caught off guard. "I'm sure I must have asked."

"No. I specifically remember thinking it odd that you knew my name."

Biting their lip, the stranger leaned farther over the fence and looked up at Vivian through a mess of fringe, "Sorry, I just feel like I know you so well already."

"How could you know me? We've only just met."

"I've read about you."

"Read about me?" Vivian asked, bewildered as sweat began to drip down the back of her neck.

"Yes, the Secret Diary of an Anonymous School Teacher. It took me ages of research to track down who you were."

Vivian shook her head, she'd never shared her diary with anyone, "I think you've mistaken me for someone else."

"You mentioned I was handsome, which I find quite generous. Though I do agree that I have a 'roguish nature'."

"Who told you that?" Taking a step back from the fence, Vivian furtively looked around to see if anyone else was around.

The stranger pulled out a small linen-bound volume and held it out, "I read it, I told you."

The cover was her favorite dusty rose color, with flowers embossed in gold foil. She wanted to snatch it from the stranger's hand, but she was afraid of what it might contain. Her throat was dry as she asked, "Those were my private…"

Opening the small book, the stranger flipped through a few pages before quoting, "*The stranger was quite handsome. Roguish even. I could see them being in the pictures. Maybe, sucking on a cigarette or cigar while they gaze longingly after their lost love. Maybe opposite Dietrich, though she's been doing cabaret.*"

The stranger looked back up at Vivian, shifting closer to her so they were almost nose to nose, "I would have loved to meet Marlene Dietrich by the way."

"No, you don't understand. That's from my diary. How could something from my diary be in a book?" she asked, trying to peer at the pages.

"It was published by the family after the author disappeared. They hoped she might come back if they published it."

"You're talking about it as if that all happened in the past."

"It did. For me, 1952 is in the past. Some of the content was quite scandalous. Highsmith's book comes out later that year and Wilde is still being censored."

Vivian could feel her breath catch in her chest, "It's 1951."

"I know." Smiling sadly the stranger nodded, "I realize this is confusing, but I think we were destined to meet."

"Destined?"

"You've always dreamed of having more than what you can have here. More than being a school teacher for the rest of your life. More than watching your friends and family be happy while your own happiness is out of reach. That isn't fair to you."

Swallowing hard, Vivian held her hand out for the book, "Let me see it."

The stranger gave her a nervous look, "I may not be able to find my way back without it."

Somehow she knew the stranger was telling the truth, but Vivian had to see it for herself. Wrapping one hand around the slim volume, she slipped a sprig of rosemary into the breast pocket of the stranger's shirt.

She was standing at the gate alone again, the diary clutched tightly to her chest.

Rain dripped down the window panes as Vivian watched the garden mournfully from the window seat. There'd been no sign of the stranger since they'd disappeared. The rose-colored diary had been sitting like a dreaded letter on the window seat since that day. She hadn't had the courage to open it yet. Thunder crashed outside followed a moment later by a streak of lightning across the sky. The lights flickered. A second rumble of thunder sounded just above the townhouse, rattling the windows in their frames as the power went out.

Pulling a knit shawl around her shoulders, Vivian grumbled and got up to find a candle. The landlord had been promising to look at the wiring for over a year, but they somehow still hadn't gotten to it. She was tired of her power going out during every storm. It wasn't a feature of old houses that she loved.

Lighting a few candles, Vivian settled back into the window seat and gingerly picked up the little diary. It was worn, but still in good condition, even with the yellowed pages. She traced the foil roses and lavender on the cover, and with a sigh, opened the book to the title page.

Diary of a School Teacher was written in a rather plain typesetting, with 'by anonymous' listed underneath. In her own neatly swirling handwriting, an inscription was written out: To my love, Em H. Orinn, in this life and forever, thank you for stealing me away, Viv.

Her heart nearly skipped a beat as she read through the inscription again and again. Em. Could that be the stranger? Had they been given the book second hand? Flipping to the next page in search of the publication information she found a sprig of rosemary was pressed between the pages. It still smelt faintly of that earthy fragrance.

The publication date was listed as 1952, just as the stranger had said. It had to be some form of elaborate joke. Maybe a colleague who thought it was funny. Or meant to torment her by letting her know they knew her secret.

She flipped through the diary, trying to ignore the strangeness of seeing her own thoughts and fears printed on the page. Each entry begins with the hopes of being swept away by a knight with shining armor to a better life. Skipping to the final entry, she realized it was dated April 30th, 1951, two days from now.

Those of you reading this diary may be confused about this final entry. I frankly never expected to compose a farwell in this form. Unfortunately the best I can do is to leave these pages to be found later.

I never intended any of this diary to be made public, especially as most people would not approve of certain aspects of my life. However I do think it's important for some people to read about how I existed in such a time. How my blossoming love for someone different, from the expected, isn't wrong. Know that I'm now happily in a place far away from the little town I was living in.

I don't want anyone to be concerned for me. Please know that Em fully intends to take good care of me. And know that I finally have my garden.

To anyone that needs to hear this, you are not alone. You are loved. You belong. Your true home may be beyond the stars, far from where you pictured it, but know you have one. Leave your window open, and adventure will find you.

Lovingly, V.

The diary had greatly unsettled her. She'd nearly thrown it into the fireplace several times, but each time, Vivian's heart ached. Pacing back and forth in her tiny sitting room lit by a few candles, she tried to determine what to do.

She could leave.

It was possible that she was in danger. Killing someone that was different was definitely not unheard of. But another part of her yearned for the stranger to return.

Besides, where would she go? The next train to the city wouldn't leave until Monday. And her parents didn't have a phone yet, so she'd have to call the general store down the road from them and hope to reach them. Leaving would mean explaining. Revealing her secrets. Hoping that they would still love her, though she suspected they would.

Rain pattered at the window almost sounding like someone tapping gently on the glass. Going to the window seat, she double-checked the latch, making certain it was locked tight. But as she looked out into the dark, stormy evening, a thought struck her, "I could stay here, go to my parents, stay miserable or—"

Windows could be portals to other worlds, just like wardrobes or looking glasses. Hand on the latch, she felt a bit like Wendy, torn between the idea of some fantastic adventure, and the reality of growing up.

Running to the kitchen, Vivian pulled the battered, leather-bound notebook that contained her recipes from a shelf. It was her most precious possession. When she returned to the window seat, she stepped up onto the seat and closed her eyes as she pulled it open. Instead of a cold, wet burst of air as she'd expected, there was a pleasantly warm breeze that smelt of coffee and fire smoke.

Her tiny garden was nowhere to be seen, replaced by a room she'd never seen before. The walls were lined with bookshelves packed with books and knickknacks, an oversized desk was covered in clutter, mugs teetering precariously on stacks of papers. A green reading lamp glowed softly, providing the only light in the room. And asleep in the chair behind the desk, was a stranger, a book resting open across their chest, glasses sliding down their nose. It felt like she was discovering the Darling nursery in the quiet twilight hours just before waking from the dream of Neverland.

Glancing back into her little apartment, she could see that her sitting room was fading a bit at the edges. Just like the bicycle. And the stranger. She bent down to pick up the diary, then set one foot onto the cushioned window seat in the new room.

The threadbare cushion and the wooden seat underneath were solid, even though she'd half expected it to fall away when she put her weight on it. As she put her other foot down, the wood creaked and the person at the desk stirred.

Wincing, she moved carefully, trying not to make any more noise as she approached the sleeping stranger. Their hair stood up as if it hadn't been brushed in days. Dozens of books were open across the desk, with notes scribbled on scraps of paper. Vivian could feel tears welling up in her eyes when she saw the sprig of rosemary perched on top of another stack of books in a coffee mug.

She knew she couldn't be dreaming, the wool rug under her toes felt too real. The excitement of a new life was threatening to turn to dread as the realness began to sink in. Could she go back? If things turned out to be worse? What were the long-term effects of such travel? Looking down at the diary she was clutching tightly in her hands, she took a deep breath and ripped the final pages from the book before rushing back to the window.

It felt like the right thing to do, leaving the pages back in her sitting room in 1951. As she flung them back through the window, she watched as they floated to the ground like leaves. Spring was for new beginnings, new life, taking chances. As Austen had written, *'Let other pens dwell on guilt and misery.'* She'd taken the leap and couldn't bear to regret it now. Not with everything being an unknown moving forward.

"Why are you crying?" the stranger asked their voice hoarse from sleep.

Vivian turned to face them, suddenly feeling like an interloper, "I'm not sure if I'm sad or relieved."

"Maybe you're a little bit of both?" they said, still rubbing the sleep from their eyes as they got up, setting aside their book.

"You didn't come back."

"Doorways to other worlds have a mind of their own I'm afraid."

"I read the rest of it," Vivian said, holding up the diary, "And then..."

"You found your way here?"

"I guess. Maybe it's right that I had to find

you.”

Picking up the mug with the sprig of rosemary, the stranger twirled it around, “This might have helped.”

Laughing, Vivian wiped at her eyes, wishing the tears would stop, “Like some kind of token? Calling me here?”

The stranger shrugged, setting the mug aside again, “You never know. Sometimes you’re chasing a rabbit into Wonderland—”

“And sometimes you meet a stranger in your garden.”

“You could help with my garden. If you want to stay that is?”

Looking back at the window, her sitting room had almost completely faded away now, resembling a chalk painting melting in the rain, “If you’ll have me.”

“Of course, I’ll have you, Miss Vivian.”

“It’s Viv,” she insisted, not minding that the portal might be gone for good. The library’s window looked over a brick path that led to a grand, fenced-in garden along the estate’s south side. She already had great plans for it, including a good deal of rosemary.

They smiled, “My name is Em.”

Vivian nodded, wrapping her arms around Em’s neck, “I know.”

kingdom FALL

Cay Fletcher

KINGDOM FALL

IMRE & MAAKET

IMRE WENT THROUGH THE ceremony of dressing for the occasion, ignoring the darkness that pressed in through the floor-to-ceiling windows of the King's chambers. He wasn't one for finery, but he knew that he needed to look presentable at least. Like a king should when walking into danger. Events had been coming to a head for some time now and he had taken the throne knowing that the day would come when the violence would reach the palace walls. Stars had aligned, signs could be seen in the faint ring around the moon, and the heavy rainfall had all signaled to his advisers that things would end badly. They'd warned and pleaded for him to flee before they abandoned the palace themselves in the dead of night. He could hardly blame them.

The fewer pieces on the board at the end, the less bloodshed there would be.

Stacks of military reports covered his oversized desk, dressers, tables, and piled against armchairs, eclipsing the few memos that had been drawn up about canceling the harvest festivals. As much as Imre had wanted to give the people hope, it wasn't the time for celebrations. Maaket's army, a collection of mercenaries and sailors from what the reports could tell, had landed on the coast months prior and made quick progress through the heart of the kingdom. Imre's standing orders were to not engage. The last thing Imre wanted were more dead soldiers, farmers, and children. So far, casualties had been minimal, but that still meant he'd had to send poppies back to families, rather than their loved ones.

He wondered how Maaket had escaped the shipwreck, and assassination attempts. And why it had taken him so long to fight his way back home. But those answers weren't in the reports that littered his study, and Imre doubted he would ever know what the man had been doing for the past seven years when it had been hard enough to discover that he was even alive.

Glancing in a mirror, his gaunt reflection

stared back at him. He was exhausted after months of war meetings that left little time for social reforms or support for farmers and their families. A kingdom was far more than those that marched off to war. There needed to be something to come back to once the dust settled and the flags were moved along new borders.

Combing a hand through his limp hair, he glared at the crown resting on its ceremonial stand. A grab for what amounted to a lump of gold and jewels was what had started him down this path. It was the reason he was about to lose everything he'd ever worked for. And everyone he'd held dear. He hadn't even been King for more than a year, and yet the consequences of the last few years were barreling towards the end.

As the candlelight flickered in the background, Imre tried to banish the thoughts that crept into the back of his mind when he was alone. Looking at the grand bed, he stared at the stains that had never come out of the wooden headboard. He could taste the horrible coppery flavor of blood in his mouth and found his hands shaking. Maybe if things had been different, he would have had time to heal. And he wouldn't feel disgusted at every mention of the former king.

Going to the window, Imre shoved open the glass and took a deep breath. Usually, the scent of flowers permeated everything this time of year, but the chilly spring air carried the smell of smoke and rain along with it. He hated that the kingdom was in such disarray.

Going back to the mirror, he slipped on a simple tunic, followed by a leather vest covered in pockets and various attachments. A souvenir from his days as a mage, following along behind armies to dispense remedies and ease the pain of those too far gone to help. It all seemed like ages ago. Most of the pockets were empty now, but some things contained within might still be useful in the hours to come. He pulled out a vial of poppy syrup and examined it. It was enough to kill a grown man, but he sincerely hoped things wouldn't come to that.

He tugged on the weighty, regal robes, dark as the night sky and embellished with the finest gold and silver embroidery. He hated the color, and the emblems stitched into the robes, reminding him of the dead men that had held the crown before him, making his skin crawl. They felt like the man's fingers were still moving over him. Part of him wished he'd burnt them. But they were, unfortunately, as necessary to symbolize the current monarch as the crown.

Around his neck, he hung a pendant of delicately carved red stone, a touchstone for his magic. It had been formed into the nearly transparent petals of a poppy. A gift from his dearest friend, from what seemed like a lifetime ago. This time of year the hills were stained with a rainbow of poppies.

He looked over his reflection one final time as he placed the heavy crown on his head. The man in front of him was hardly recognizable as the mage who had grown up alongside the princes. Imre had never even dreamed of the crown or ruling or being responsible for an entire kingdom. He'd just wanted to help people. And even though he'd done his best, he still felt like a failure.

His footsteps echoed against the empty stone halls, as the robes slunk along behind him. Outside, the once-prosperous kingdom was burning, ash and smoke carried on the wind up the hill to the palace filling it with an acrid smell. The farmers, terrified of what would happen if they were found to be cooperative with his rule, had decided it best to just burn their livelihoods. Imre had begged his advisers to help quell their fears, but with time so short, not much could be done.

He didn't bother to light the torches as he approached the throne room. It would be more fitting to sit and wait for his adversary in the dark. Optics were important in the reporting and recording of such confrontations and tales would be told of the moments yet to unfurl for generations.

Queer Windows

The chill sank into his bones, even with the thick robes wrapping around his shoulders and trailing behind him. It was just beginning to get warmer, with the wet spring days stretching into the lazy warmth of summer. At least the rain would help contain the fires. Though it might be too late for farmers to save their crops. Only time would tell. A good minister of agriculture would be able to help with their recovery, sourcing seeds from other kingdoms and working to trade for what they needed to survive another year.

There were no guards, attendants, or advisers present, just himself waiting, his dagger slipped amongst the folds of his robes. The various parts of his plan were falling into place, one by one. As the kingdom's soldiers had allowed their attackers to pass by, the palace's defenses had been lowered and everyone had been evacuated. Minimizing the damage had always been his priority. He'd let them back him into a corner, and now it was time to allow the endgame he'd planned to unfold.

As the first light broke, he could hear heavy footsteps approaching the grand entrance to the throne room. His fingers traced the groves of the poppy pendant's petals, a soothingly familiar reminder that death was always near at hand. Keeping his expression neutral, he watched as Maaket pushed through the doors, his men trailing a few steps behind him. Imre could feel his breath catch in his throat as the man he'd known so long ago strode across the marble tiles, looking far more handsome than he had once been. Maaket was no longer the lanky boy he had sparred against in the courtyard. His dark hair hung over his eyes, sweat dripping down his face as he stopped in front of the throne. Somehow even dirt and soot couldn't diminish his beauty.

Imre remembered the moment he'd fallen for the other man, looking up at him, flat on his back after being knocked down in a sparring match. Maaket's eyes had been so kind as he had offered him a hand up and helped him correct his stance.

"Seems you've found your way home finally, Maaket."

"Surrender," Maaket said, his voice commanding even though Imre could hear his tiredness seeping into it. He motioned to his men to stand down.

"You've taken the palace," Imre replied, keeping half an eye on the others Maaket had brought with him. "What is there left to surrender?"

"Yourself, Imre. Stand down and you can keep your life," Maaket asked again. He had never accepted surrender during their sparring matches. It struck Maaket as unfair somehow, though he'd never explained how to Imre.

"You've been away for almost seven years and many things have changed. I won't just surrender. You'll have to take the throne from me," he had practiced the words, knowing the time to recite them would come sooner or later.

Maaket shook his head, "We were friends once, Imre."

Imre swallowed and tried not to let his true reaction to the statement show on his face, "Once?"

"Yes, once upon a time. But that crown doesn't belong to you."

"Doesn't it?" Imre couldn't help but smile as he touched it gently, the gold cool beneath his fingertips. It wasn't the first time power would be transferred with bloodshed, and it wasn't the last.

"You stole it. From my brother. The rightful King," Maaket said grimly, raising his sword. There was anger in his eyes. Hurt and anger. What rumors had reached him throughout the years? Imre knew that some of them had not been kind.

"Are you sure you know what happened? You have been gone for almost seven years. So much has changed since you ran off to war. You died. Your father died. And then, your brother died. But his death was necessary."

"Necessary? We grew up together! How could you be so flippant about killing him?" Maaket asked.

"I'm not being flippant, I was being practical. You were presumed dead after your ship went down. With your brother dead, I was the next in line. You made the proclamation yourself before you left. Don't you recall? Or would you have preferred the kingdom be left to rot while ministers debated who should rule it?" Imre asked.

Maaket was openly seething, "As you can see, I'm not dead. And the intent was never for you to take over the country!"

"Yes. I can see that now. It was just a pity title because there was never meant to be any hope of me achieving it. But you underestimated my ambition." he wanted to pick at the cracks in Maaket's resolve. If he wasn't going to do it on his own then Imre wasn't afraid to push. "Honestly, I'm grateful that you're alive. But, you do know that letters generally work better than military campaigns for delivering information? Then again, communication was never your strong suit, was it?"

Imre rested his elbow on the arm of the throne, looking down at Maaket, "Based on the reports, I honestly expected more men. Don't tell me they died."

"They're securing the city. Though most of the soldiers have laid down their arms without question. Because they know who the rightful ruler of this country is."

With a smile, Imre wagged his finger, "Don't tell your enemy your movements, Maaket. Even when you have them cornered. A viper will strike its hardest when it has no options. Though you would have learned that if you hadn't gone off to play war commander."

"Someone needed to lead our navy and armies. You know that," Maaket replied, exasperated.

"You could have deputized someone to lead. There were plenty of capable generals at the time," if Maaket had, maybe they could have been more than friends.

"It needed to be me."

"No! It didn't! As crown prince, you had the responsibility to be here! With your people!" Imre fired back, his voice rising, fingers gripping the worn arm of the throne.

"Those soldiers are my people too!" Maaket yelled back, "They're no different than your precious mages, or farmers, or merchants. I never wanted to fight my own people, and luckily most have surrendered before things came to blows. But some have still died, and they've died for your pride."

"I've been on those battlefields. I've washed the blood of hundreds from my hands after a battle. Don't you dare say that anyone has died because of my pride. They're dead because your brother was a power-hungry monster. The last casualty count from this offensive you've launched on your own kingdom only tallied a dozen! More of your people are going to die of starvation this winter than at the hands of your mercenaries."

The tension was palpable as Maaket's men slowly reached for their weapons. Maaket wouldn't break eye contact though, "What happened to you?"

Imre laughed, "What happened? I spent your brother's reign trying to mitigate the harm he was causing to your people. Desperately attempting to stop the wars he started and make sure there was enough food and resources to go around! A foreign campaign led by the former king's brother, returned from the dead, has not been helping my attempts at recovery. Every time I thought we were finally coming back from the brink, some new catastrophe would crop up. I've been saving this kingdom. That's what happened to me, Maaket."

"If things were so bad, then why not ask for help?" Maaket asked.

"Ask for help?" he asked, insulted that Maaket thought he hadn't, "From who? Our neighbors that Taakah spent years insulting and attacking? Trade partners, that he reneged on treaties with? Who should I have asked? Taakah dying was the end of a reign of terror."

"Don't speak about him like that," Maaket warned.

Imre rose to his full height, the dagger hidden at his side, "I'll speak about him however I like. He was a horrible king. If you'd been here, you would have done it yourself. Now, if you want to avenge him and take back what's yours, you're going to have to kill me. Are you prepared for that?"

The men Maaket had brought with him didn't lower their weapons, instead of stepping forward. Threatening him. Hoping that he would back down. To surrender like Maaket had clearly expected. But he wasn't the mage that Maaket had known since childhood anymore.

Maaket seemed to hesitate for a moment and Imre used those few seconds to wrap his hand tightly around the blade of the dagger. He was used to the pain and didn't flinch as warm blood began to soak into the robes. It was more than enough of a spark for him to wipe out every man standing before him. But that wasn't his aim. He wanted Maaket alone. To explain the last seven years to him, away from the pressures and influences of others. Raising his hand, Imre began reciting the spell under his breath almost silently. Luckily only Imre needed to hear the words.

"What's he casting?" one of Maaket's men shouted, his hand drawing back the string of his bow.

Imre stepped forward, eyes focused on the

man with the bow, daring him to fire.

"No! Wait!" Surprise flashed across Maaket's face as the arrow flew into Imre's left shoulder, knocking him back against the throne. The dagger slipped from his hands and skittered down the steps to Maaket's feet. Imre gritted his teeth against the pain, wheezing out the final words as he clutched the arm of the throne.

"You idiot! We're not supposed to kill him. You were supposed to disarm him!" another called out.

But it was too late. The spell dropped into place, locking Imre and Maaket into an impenetrable bubble of eerie darkness, cutting them off from everything else happening around them. It would stand until Imre released it, or he was killed.

Imre sank against the gilded throne on the steps of the dais. The arrow hurt far more than it should have, or maybe he'd forgotten what an arrow wound felt like since leaving the battlefield. He tenderly touched the shaft and winced as barbs released along it, lodging the arrow firmly in his shoulder.

"What are you doing? Trying to buy yourself time?"

"No."

"Your soldiers surrendered. Your advisers abandoned you. No one is coming to save you,"

Maaket told him, glancing around the confines of the bubble. The edges of it swirled like smoke, not allowing a clear view of what was happening inside. "I thought even you of all people wouldn't resort to something so cowardly."

"I ordered them to surrender. So they could look after the citizens," Imre said, ignoring the verbal jab, "I wanted a chance to talk to you."

"I have nothing more to say to you!" he yelled, whirling on Imre.

'He's so full of passion.' Imre hoped that that passion would help rebuild the kingdom for his people. Maaket bent down to pick up the dagger and frowned, his thumb running over the blood-covered blade.

"Then listen to me for once in your life!" it came out far more desperate than Imre had hoped it would. "If I'd known you were alive earlier, then I would have insisted the crown be held for you. I would have sent the armies to look for you. No one wanted Taakah to be king. But your brother insisted that you had been lost at sea. My hands were tied, both by those loyal to him in the government and because he became the heir apparent upon your death Maaket."

"You still could have waited," Maaket said.

Imre sighed, "Waited for what? Your return from the dead? All the while leaving the kingdom in shambles and open for attack by her enemies?"

"Taakah didn't need to die!"

"He declared war as soon as your father's pyre was lit. I tried to reason with him. Your father's advisers tried to. Taakah had them all exiled or killed."

"Why would he do that?"

"Because he never cared about anyone besides himself. He was a selfish tyrant who only wanted power. I need you to believe me. When have I ever lied to you, Maaket?"

"Maybe not, but how did you hold onto power if he wouldn't listen to you?"

Imre could feel ghostly fingers caressing his neck, "He liked me enough to keep me around. He wasn't exactly fond of explaining himself."

The former King had shown up in his chambers without prompting enough times for him to be fairly certain how he'd survived so long when so many others hadn't. He'd seen the way Taakah watched him, predator-like. And while things had never progressed to Taakah's liking, it only made the guilt Imre felt worse.

Maaket looked him over as if trying to tell if he was lying. It was eerily similar to how Taakah would appraise him, deciding if that would be the day he was done with him, "The country is still burning, Imre. What exactly do you think have you accomplished by taking what was never meant to be yours to begin with? "

"I bought the people time."

"Time for what?"

"To survive. Things were becoming desperate."

"There are other ways to depose a bad king, Imre! We have laws for a reason!"

"You must have missed the day in lessons where we learned that our country has never had a king successfully deposed," Imre grinned, "The council should have deposed me when you, with a rightful heir to the throne, showed up on our shores with an army. But you didn't even attempt to contact them. You'd made up your mind, that I was guilty of treason, and that the only way to take the throne back was with a show of force."

Maaket was quiet for a moment before saying, "It is treasonous to kill the ruler of the kingdom."

"Yes, it is," he could see the last crumbs of the mage Maaket had known crumble away.

"Did you kill my brother?" Maaket asked quietly.

Imre had tried to come up with so many ways to answer that question. There was no way around the truth, that he'd been the one to plunge his dagger into Taakah's chest. It had to be him. No one else had the political capital to survive past such an assassination attempt, "Yes. And I would do it again."

Maaket shook his head sadly, "You're not the same person I knew as a child."

"I had to grow up, Maaket. Just as you did."

Closing the space between them, Maaket drew his sword and pressed the edge of his blade against Imre's neck, "I can't forgive you for killing him. For becoming a traitor. A usurper."

He felt himself tremble as the cool blade rested against his skin. How he wished this reunion was something to cherish. But he couldn't see another way, even as he wished there had been time for one last embrace. As friends.

"Even if I did it to protect the kingdom you love so much? It was the right thing, at the right time," Imre asked, looking into Maaket's stormy eyes. "I was his adviser, and my sources reported rumors that you might still be alive, though no one could locate you. If you were alive, then killing him was the only way to protect you."

"How could you have been trying to protect me by *murdering* him? You thought I was dead," Maaket reminded him, pressing the edge of the sword almost hard enough to break the skin.

"He insisted they were just rumors." Imre continued, "But then I found the orders he gave to have you killed. They were in his own hand. And when I confronted him about it, he didn't deny he'd done it. Only that he regretted that his first attempt had failed. That he'd already ordered men to hunt you down," Imre swallowed, "He knew you were still alive, and yet he went through with his schemes to convince the country that you were dead. He pretended to mourn you. And everyone had bought his lies because of anyone, he would know if you were really gone, through your bond. The two of you could always tell if the other was hurt or just having a bad day."

Imre had agonized over the decision, knowing it would cause Maaket pain. Knowing his oldest friend would feel the moment his brother died.

Maaket let the blade relax against Imre's neck, "That doesn't make sense."

"You were a few minutes older. He was never going to be king unless you were dead. Even if you'd come back when he was still alive, do you think he would have let you live? How could he have explained being so wrong about you being dead?" Imre continued.

His former friend stood over him, picking through the emotions that came with the revelation that his twin wanted him dead. Imre's arm and shoulder were beginning to go numb, "If you kill me now, his memory won't be tarnished. You can explain that Taakah was just protecting you while you were at war. And you could still return a hero of the kingdom."

"I don't understand, why would you care about his memory?"

"Because he was your brother. And no matter what has happened, I know you cared for him."

"Being my brother doesn't excuse any of this! Or what you've done. Even if it was out of some strange sense of loyalty."

"Yes, loyalty. You always were dense," he said quietly, smiling as he tried to savor this soft moment. Imre gently touched Maaket's cheek, his blood smearing over Maaket's skin, "Just make it quick, please."

Maaket opened his mouth to respond, but closed it again, spotting the pendant hanging around Imre's neck. He reached out and ran his fingers over the delicate petals, "I gave you this to you when we were fifteen. Before I was sent to the front lines."

Imre nodded, "It saved me numerous times."

"I always thought that poppies suited you."

"Because mages dealt with so much death?"

"No, because you could return soldiers from

the brink of it."

"That's giving me too much credit" he chuckled softly. "Your father never forgave you for giving away one of the family's prized jewels. To some nobody."

"You're not a nobody. You said it yourself, you were next in line for the crown."

Wrapping his hand around Maaket's, he shook his head, "Only because you gave me that distinction."

"You're the smartest person I know. Not giving you a position as an adviser would have been criminal."

"And here I always thought it was just because you didn't want me in the line of fire anymore," Imre quipped.

"Maybe," Maaket rubbed his thumb over the stone flower again, "If you had used this, you wouldn't be injured right now."

"Stories need villains. I never had any intention of hurting you or your men."

"I've spent the last year hating you…"

"I know," the raw ire still stung Imre's heart.

"Why didn't you say something before it came to this point? You could have sent a messenger. An envoy. Anything."

"Would you have listened? You stormed in here with an army of mercenaries."

Maaket looked ashamed, "That wound isn't fatal, even if you weren't the best healer I know."

"No. It's better if you end this."

"How is losing you better?" Maaket set down his sword and started looking through the pouches and pockets on Imre's vest, "If my brother really did try to have me killed, then there's no reason I should lose you too."

Imre grabbed Maaket's hands, his own shaking, "And how will you explain that to your men?"

"You will. I'm shit at convincing people of things, remember? Besides, none of them really wanted to hurt you."

He was stunned by Maaket's response. He'd gone through every possible variable in planning his last moments, but Maaket making an about-face had seemed impossible.

Pulling a vial from one of the pockets on Imre's vest, Maaket took out the stopper and sniffed it, coughing as his lungs filled with the potent smell, "Drink this."

"I... you're supposed to kill me and take back the crown. Restore the kingdom."

Maaket blinked at Imre, "Or you could drink this, and restore the kingdom yourself. You've already been trying to."

He'd missed Maaket's no-nonsense

personality so much, "What if it doesn't work?"

"Doubting your own potion work now?" Maaket asked.

"What? No. I mean what if your men don't believe you. What if the people revolt?"

"Then we'll deal with that as it comes. Together. Now drink the damn potion before I force it down your throat," Maaket told him, handing him the bottle.

Part of Imre expected some kind of trick. If it was Taakah sitting beside him, then his expectations would likely be realized, but Maaket had always been loyal and kind-hearted. His gentleness had always drawn people to him. Maybe it had been too much to think that Maaket would kill him just out of anger. Tipping the vial back, Imre swallowed the liquid and gripped Maaket's shoulder tightly, "Pull out the arrow."

Maaket didn't give him time to prepare himself before snapping the shaft of the arrow in half and pulling out the end with the head. The barbs tore at his shoulder, splintering pain shooting through him, but the wound began to close as soon as the arrow was removed. Meeting Maaket's eyes, Imre started to let the bubble slip away.

"Wait, Imre…" Maaket said, squeezing his hand, "Is that it?"

"It is. Why?"

"I guess I was expecting a confession."

Imre let the confusion show on his face as the bubble melted away, "A confession of what?"

Maaket's men stood at the ready around the edge of the bubble, but even though they were clearly waiting for instructions, Maaket didn't pay them any mind. Instead, he leaned over Imre and pressed their lips together briefly.

"I'm not so dense that I don't know how you feel."

A knot was forming in the back of Imre's throat as he fought back the urge to cry. The sun had begun to peek out from behind the rain clouds and was streaming into the throne room as Maaket stood up and held a hand out for him. He'd hoped that the sun would come out today, a good omen for the future of the kingdom.

"Men, let me introduce King Imre, my oldest friend," Maaket told them as he pulled Imre close.

"He's smarter than what you told us," one of the men said. "Surprised he didn't off your brother sooner."

There was an uncomfortable beat of silence before Maaket said, "Luckily Imre isn't normally the killing type."

"You talked about me?" Imre asked in a hushed whisper.

"Of course."

The man with the bow was avoiding Imre and Maaket's gaze, "I didn't mean to fire that arrow."

Maaket nodded, "Well hopefully you won't have to shoot anyone anytime soon."

"It looks as if our suspicions were correct then?" the leader of the group asked.

"I guess they were."

"What suspicions?" Imre asked as the men all lowered their weapons.

"There were rumors that the ship wrecking was no accident. Unfortunately, it wrecked in hostile territory. Maaket here spent a couple of years just trying to fight his way to somewhere he wouldn't be killed for being a foreigner."

"You knew then?" Imre asked, turning to Maaket. He would have to interrogate Maaket later for the full story. Seven years was a lot to catch up on.

"The idiot really thought you'd turned traitor, my liege. We convinced him not to level the palace and talk with you to figure out what had happened. Especially given how the soldiers all laid down their arms when we arrived. That in itself would have been a bit suspicious."

Imre punched Maaket's shoulder, "What was your plan if I used magic against you?"

"Uh…" Maaket rubbed his shoulder and

looked to his men for assistance but all he received was a few knowing chuckles. "All that's in the past now. Besides, we can be together now."

Taking a deep breath, Imre shook his head slowly, "We have a lot to go over before 'being together'. You have a kingdom to run. Have you even thought about what to do about the fields that are currently on fire?"

"I figured you could keep running it. After all, you're already King," Maaket replied.

"You lot, please go find the captain of the guard and ensure that water lines are set up to put out the fires. I need to deal with him," Imre ordered, glaring at Maaket.

"As you wish, my liege," the leader said with a bow and a bit of a chuckle. "Good luck with him."

When they were alone, Imre untied the heavy robes and let them drop from his shoulders. The slice on his hand was already healed, but his shoulder was taking longer to knit itself back together. He felt like he could sleep for days as the anxiety and adrenaline drained from his body.

Maaket took his hand and walked him back up the dais before dropping to one knee, his head bowing, "You're the better king, Imre."

Imre wasn't used to looking down at Maaket, "Get up."

"Not until you agree to keep the crown."

Pulling the crown from his head, Imre held it out to Maaket, "I never wanted it."

"I didn't either. Why do you think I volunteered to go lead our armies? You're so much better at planning and knowing the right move. You probably planned out a hundred ways this could have gone today."

"Except how things happened," Imre admitted, slumping into the throne.

Maaket took the crown from Imre's hand and replaced it on his head, grinning, "It looks good on you."

"It's ostentatious."

Shrugging, Maaket leaned down and kissed Imre again, "You can always have a new one made. A circlet of jeweled poppies maybe?"

A shiver ran through Imre as Maaket's knee pressed between his legs, "That's a waste of resources."

"See, I think you're the best king we could ask for."

Imre wrapped his arms around Maaket's neck and pulled him closer. He'd imagined what it would feel like to die. Whether it would be quick or drag on painfully. But like so many other plans, he wouldn't ever know the conclusion to his worst predictions of that day.

"Well, then your king would like you to shut up and keep kissing him."

Lady of Spring

Cay Fletcher

LADY OF SPRING

STALKS OF TALL GRASS rippled under Vinq's fingertips as she walked through the field below her village. In the late summer and fall she'd make sure to shake seeds from their pods, and the dried husks of flowers as she walked so that the meadow would return even more beautifully the next spring. The sun hadn't fully woken up yet, but the birds singing to each other always acted as her wake-up call. She took a deep breath of the sweet, frosty, morning air, savoring the smell of the inevitable rain showers.

Mornings, before the sun spread across the valley, were her favorite times. She could wander the meadow alone, ensuring the flowers unfurled their petals. Or go down to the stream to tickle the tadpoles and find polished stones to add to her collection in the garden.

Reaching the top of one of the hills, she laid down, letting the dew droplets sprinkle down over her face. The last stars twinkled as they slowly faded from view and the wind rushed over the hilltop, making it sing. She feared that this might be the last morning like it. Her last morning completely free of responsibilities, expectations, and a future she wasn't certain of.

"Mother, what if I don't want to go through with the ceremony?" she whispered, letting the wind carry her words away on the breeze.

Sometimes there was an answer, but as she laid there, feeling the chilly earth underneath her, Vinq couldn't hear any response. If her mother had been there, maybe she would have been able to offer some guidance. But as it stood, Vinq only had her older siblings, who were only occasionally useful in the advice department. Sometimes she felt they misunderstood her on purpose.

Picking a few blades of grass, Vinq began plaiting them together. Every so often she wove a wildflower into the green band. Ilo hated such crafty little trinkets, which had always seemed at odds with her position as a priestess. Most of the priestesses loved nature and often incorporated plants into ceremonies, but Ilo's skin broke out in hives whenever she touched anything green.

Quin, on the other hand, was always asking Vinq to bring armfuls of wildflowers back from her days wandering the meadows. He loved showcasing the bright colors in his art, using them for dyes, or drying and grinding them to dust for paint. Everyone in the village assumed that they got along well, but they were always at odds. Quin was far more disciplined than Vinq ever could be and her messes and general lack of care about her appearance drove him crazy.

Instead, it was their eldest sibling, Hind, that Vinq got along with best. He was easygoing and didn't force her to come inside when it rained. Or admonished her when she wanted to play with the fireflies on warm summer evenings. He'd sneak her sweet treats and even let her keep the lizard she'd found when she was younger as a pet.

She wouldn't have time for most of that when she was assigned her position within the village though.

Closing her eyes, she listened to the breeze and the birds chattering. The robins and jays were fighting over breakfast and in the distance, she could hear the cry of the crows echoing from across the valley. She would miss her morning escapes.

The close crunching of steps caught her

attention and she sat up to spot Hind surveying the meadow. His duties with the chief usually had him up early, but today he was supposed to supervise her. She watched him pick a few early poppies as he searched for her. Vinq stayed low, like an animal lying in wait for its prey, as Hind drew closer.

As she crouched down, Vinq gently took one of the stalks of grass nearby and blew at the dew that was still clinging to the top of it. The tiny drops of water floated off the grass and onto the wind, towards her brother. Dew from other plants followed, like a swarm of insects until the collection of thin water droplets collided with Hind's face with a splash.

Vinq giggled as he wiped the water from his face with a sleeve.

"I knew you'd be out here somewhere. Come on Vinq!"

"Sorry, there is no Vinq here. Only the meadow goblin," she replied, dropping her voice.

"Even meadow goblins have to go through the crowning ceremony," he crossed his arms.

"I'd like some proof of that."

Hind smiled, "Ilo went through hers."

Vinq nearly toppled over from laughter, "I'm telling her you said that!"

"No, you won't. Now come along, there's a lot to do today."

"I still have to fetch an oak apple. I'll be just a moment - I've done that loads of times."

Hind clicked his tongue, "You still need to get ready."

"I'm not wearing that lacy dress," Vinq assured him, getting up from her hiding spot and not bothering to brush the grass and dirt from herself.

"Ilo spent a lot of time on it."

Vinq shrugged, "It's white. I'll never wear it again. She can keep it."

Hind sighed, "We can talk about that later."

"Has mother talked to you recently? In your dreams?"

Shaking his head, Hind tucked the poppies he'd picked behind one of Vinq's pointed ears, "No. Have you been asking her questions?"

"Yes."

"Then maybe it's something you already know the answer to. I'll race you to the oak tree."

She was a bit disappointed by Hind's explanation, even though it seemed annoyingly reasonable. The Head Priestess often warned about seeking answers from beyond rather than coming to the answer on her own. Even if some could converse with those who had passed in dreams, sometimes it was better to look internally.

"Okay, but no cheating and none of your

magic.”

"Sounds fair,” Hind said before taking off towards the huge oak tree ahead of Vinq.

Taking off after Hind, the wind whistled through the fresh shoots of grass as Vinq flew up the hill at top speed. Her bare feet hardly even touched the ground as she focused on reaching the old oak that stood on the crest of the hill before her older brother. Reaching out her fingers, an amused chuckle distracted her before she could touch the tree's bark. She collided with the tree with a thud and grumbled.

"I told you, no magic allowed Hind.”

"I didn't use magic,” Hind said, offering her a hand.

"Oh? Then how did you beat me?”

"Quick-foot potion,” Hind said as he casually pulled a flask from his tunic and sipped at it.

"Potions are magic!”

"You said 'none of our magic' could be used. I didn't make the potion.”

Vinq punched his arm lightheartedly, "Jerk. You can't cheat a lady. So that was the last time!”

"Lady? I don't know, I still have a few hours until you're one of those.”

Looking up at the oak's boughs, Vinq listened to wind whispering through the valley, "As soon as the light fades from the valley and the first bonfire of summer is lit."

"Nervous?"

Vinq snorted, "About the ceremony? Of course not."

"I heard Mari is going to be performing the ceremony," Hind said with a grin.

"Wha–what? Where did you hear that?" Vinq grabbed her brother's arms shook him in disbelief, the tips of her pointed ears growing warm, "But she's in line to become the high priestess. And I'm just…me!"

Hind shrugged, "The chief mentioned it last night. Special request I guess."

"No, no, no…my clothes aren't nice enough. I haven't even memorized what I'm going to say yet!"

"I thought you weren't nervous."

"I wasn't when it was just going to be some priestess that I don't know. Or Ilo. But Mari is…"

"What?"

"Perfect!"

"No one is perfect."

"She is. Even more perfect than Ilo. She always looks beautiful, not a single hair out of place. And when she went through her ceremony everyone knew that she'd be selected as a priestess. Besides isn't she too young to be doing ceremonies already?"

"She's a fast learner, I guess."

"Great, so I get to fail miserably in front of everyone. And everyone will know it's my fault because Mari certainly won't make any mistakes."

"No one 'fails' their coming of age ceremony. You can't fail it."

"I bet I can be the first," Vinq argued.

Hind shook his head, "You'll be fine. Now are you going to keep complaining, or are you going to climb this tree?"

"Okay, okay."

Grabbing the flask from her brother, Vinq downed a gulp of the honey wine. She still had to climb the damn oak tree and find an oak apple for the ceremony that evening. Running a hand through her short-cropped hair, Vinq circled the tree, looking for the best way up the stout trunk. She'd climbed her fair share of trees in the past, but the oak was its own unique challenge as its bark was worn smooth from centuries of young people climbing it in search of the perfect oak apple for their coming of age ceremonies. She found a knob that she could use as a handhold and hauled herself upwards, her toes finding any crevice they could for support.

"Careful!" Hind called up at her as she made it to the tree's first group of branches. "I don't want to have to patch up your face before the ceremony!"

Vinq grumbled, "I'll break your face if you keep distracting me!"

There were a few smaller oak apples just out of reach on the lowest branches, but Vinq wanted to be certain that Mari would be impressed. So she kept climbing, clinging to every branch like a lifeline as she climbed higher and higher. She didn't dare look down, not until she had her prize, the largest oak apple she'd ever seen. It was growing from the side of a flimsy branch that stretched out beyond most of the others.

Magic wasn't allowed to obtain an oak apple, even if the candidate had already begun developing some. The rule was to make certain the task was on an even playing field for everyone. Vinq didn't mind completing this part of the feat, but she also hated the idea of falling out of the tree while doing it.

Taking stock of the best way to retrieve the oak apple she'd chosen, Vinq began inching along a sturdier branch below her prize, using the higher branch like a rope. As she moved farther from the trunk of the tree, she began to feel the branch below her feet sag. She willed the branch to hold under her weight. If the branch broke, it would have been a simple thing to fix if she'd been allowed magic. Repairing a branch, just meant encouraging the fibers to weave back together. There were still a few yards to go before she'd be able to reach the oak apple though. Testing the lower branch by bobbing up and down on it, she decided to keep moving, one foot in front of the other as the branch sagged even lower.

The oak apple was almost within reach when Vinq heard the crack of the branch she was standing on. She froze waiting to see if it would stabilize. Another crack shook the branch as she clung to the one above her, then scrambled forward, snatching the oak apple off the branch as it fell away underneath her. She felt the oak apple give in her hand, but couldn't worry about if she'd crushed it or not while she was flailing in the tree branches. With a yelp, she clung to the branch above her head as the one below her feet crashed to the ground.

"You okay up there Vinq?" her brother called up.

"Yup! Just testing my route down!" Vinq yelled as she swung her body back and forth in an attempt to reach another branch. Hurling herself forward, she grabbed at the next branch in reach, wrapping her arms around it tightly.

Muttering her thanks to the tree under her breath, Vinq slowly inched back to the trunk. She took a moment to examine the slightly smushed oak apple before shoving it into a pocket. The climb down was quicker than the climb up especially with being able to drop to the ground from one of the lower branches.

Vinq stumbled a few steps before grinning triumphantly at Hind, "I just picked the biggest oak apple you've ever seen."

"Oh?" he asked with a yawn.

"Yup."

"Great, we need to get back to the house so you can get ready then."

"Can't I just hang out here?"

Hind gave her a knowing look, "Quin and Ilo promised to help you get ready. It wouldn't be fair to them to ignore that assistance."

"But I would feel more prepared if I could just, you know, relax in the meadow."

"You still have your promise to memorize. But, if things are finished early, then maybe you can relax a bit before the ceremony."

Vinq sighed, glancing up at the large oak tree longingly. Falling asleep in its arms would be far better than dealing with Ilo's constant patronizing, or Quin's nervous pampering.

Vinq could hardly sit still while her brother

Quin tried to tame her hair. Ilo was busy trying to find the perfect lilies to add to her willow branch crown, while not touching them as much as possible. Potential candidates were strewn across the kitchen table, with the discard pile growing larger and larger.

"How do you have leaves in your hair still?" Quin asked, exasperated as he yanked a comb out of her dark, tangles.

"I did just finish climbing a tree," Vinq replied, hugging the back of the chair she was sitting in, her eyes wandering over the hills through the kitchen window.

"The goal was to find an oak apple, not bring the whole tree back with you," Hind said, amused.

"At least I didn't fall out of the tree," she snapped back.

"True. The bar is pretty low," Hind said, ducking out of range as Vinq tried to throw one of the discard lilies at him.

Quin sighed, gently placing his hands on Vinq's shoulders in an attempt to relax her, "You should be focusing on what you're going to say and the rest of the ceremony. Ignore him."

Vinq deflated, resting her chin on the chair back, "There's no way I can come up with something good before tonight. Why does the ceremony have to be in front of the whole village? Can't everyone stay home? It'll be raining anyway."

Wrapping his arms around her, Quin kissed the top of her head, "You'll do fine. Just go through what you have so far. And it won't rain, the sky is blue as a forget-me-not."

"Isn't it supposed to be private? Between you and the priestess?" their sister Ilo asked.

Hind shrugged, "It is, but everyone runs their promise by someone else beforehand."

Ilo clicked her tongue, "Maybe one person, not a full room of people."

"Family is 'people' now?" Hind asked.

"Of course we're people, what else would we be?" Ilo said attaching the final lily to the woven willow crown. "This is done. I need to go wash my hands before my arms are covered in a disgusting rash."

Vinq stuck out her tongue as Ilo left the kitchen, the golden child, always the epitome of perfect. She'd been the first pick for a position with the priestesses while Vinq wasn't the first pick for anything. She was the plainest, the wildest, and the last to move from being a child to an adult.

"Don't pay her any attention," Hind said in a bored tone.

"Do I ever?" Vinq got up, grabbing the crown and looking it over, "Don't these lilies seem silly? I think we should have chosen something else.”

“Lilies are traditional for spring,” Quin insisted.

“When have I ever been traditional?”

“Never, fortunately,” Hind said with a grin, “The lilies are pretty though. They’ll look nice in the firelight.”

“Unless it rains.”

“Stop saying that,” Quin said as he began cleaning up the discarded lilies.

“Are you superstitious now?” Vinq asked in an amused tone, glancing out the window again. Maybe she could encourage some rain so fewer people would show up, “And maybe I want it to rain. I should go find a frog before the ceremony.”

Quin gave her a horrified look and said in a pained tone, “Please don’t roll in the mud. We just got your hair tamed. And you really should try on your dress so I can make sure the hem looks right.”

“I bet the mud would do me some good!” Vinq said as she bounded out of the little kitchen and out into the sunny, bustling, afternoon. Various people greeted her as she ran as fast as her feet would take her to the stream that flowed below the village. Their good wishes burned in her ears as she tried to escape the knowledge that she would end the night forever changed.

Her eyes were blurry with unshed tears as

the stream's cold water splashed her feet. She would lose her carefree days of laying in the meadow. Or wandering the woods aimlessly. Growing up meant structure. It was a promise made to the community to engage and support and be a part of the larger whole. And Vinq wasn't ready to let her freedom slip away.

"Is it wrong to want to keep being me?"

Sitting in the mud at the edge of the stream, Vinq picked up a smooth stone, "Who will sing to you every day? Or play in the stream? Or hunt down frogs to bring the rain?"

The low buzz of insects and the slosh of the stream didn't answer. She laid backward, the mud squishing out from under her, the reeds and grass bending as she spread out her arms. There was a quiet rebellion in spending her last few hours before dark laying half in the stream, away from the preparations and bustle of her family and the rest of the village. It's not as if she'd planned to avoid all the primping, even though she'd hated the idea of it. She'd resigned to following the rules, like everyone before her.

Pulling the oak apple from her pocket, Vinq held it above her head, turning it over in her hands. She was supposed to dry it out before the ceremony so it could be turned into ink. But what if she came unprepared? As far as Vinq knew, no one had ever gone to their ceremony unprepared. Everyone else, including her older siblings, had been excited to join the adults and be given responsibilities.

Vinq closed her eyes, letting the sun dry the mud into flaky chunks on her skin. The water quietly bubbled over her feet. She let all of that lull her to sleep. What sort of magic would she gain? Was it worth it? Would Mari, or the rest of the village think less of her if it wasn't something impressive? And if they did think less of her, was that a bad thing? Did it matter in the long run?

She could feel her mind drifting along with the sweet smell of the wind rolling over the hills. The part of her that knew she shouldn't allow herself to fall asleep was quickly banished by the warm embrace of dreams. Someone was gently combing their fingers through her hair as she let sleep wash over her.

"What are you dreaming of, young one?" a familiar, warm voice asked her.

Vinq's eyes felt so heavy she couldn't open them to see the form of her mother leaning over her, "My coming of age ceremony."

"That's exciting. What magic are you hoping to be given?"

"I don't know. I haven't really thought about that."

"*Why not? Isn't there something you'd like to do?*"

"I like my life now. I don't want to change."

"*This stream wasn't always here, but you still love to spend time around it. Change isn't always a bad thing. And sometimes you become a person you like even more with change.*"

"But what if I have to spend the rest of my life grinding flour? Or working the forge? Or sewing or weaving?"

"*I'm certain that the priestesses would take your love of nature into account.*"

"But if they don't?"

She felt a gentle, comforting squeeze at her hand, "*I can't alleviate your fears. But I can assure you, that even if you are given a life that you maybe don't like or understand, you will never lose your love for the natural world. You'll always be welcome in the streams, and to climb trees and lay in the meadows. You are you, and those that love you, love all the parts of you.*"

"I wish I could just stay here."

"*Then you wouldn't be able to share your gifts with everyone else.*"

"I feel more at home here."

"*Perhaps leaving your place of comfort would help you gain some confidence?*"

"It could, I guess."

"*You'll never know until you try.*"

Cold drops of rain woke Vinq where she'd fallen asleep by the stream. The croak of a nearby frog rang in her ears as she blinked the sleep from her eyes and pushed herself up. It was almost fully dark and she could see the glow of the bonfire off in distance. She didn't have time to go home and change, or even wash. Pushing herself up, Vinq started towards the bonfire.

She slipped on the grass several times as she approached the gathering. Hind spotted her first, stopping her just outside the ring of waiting villagers.

"You're late," he chastised her gently, using his thumb to wipe some dirt from her chin.

"I know! I know!" Vinq was glad that he didn't comment on the mud in her hair, or how her clothes were soaked and dirty.

"Don't worry, you'll do just fine," he placed the woven willow crown sans the lilies that had been attached to it earlier on her head. "I figured this was more you."

Vinq wrapped her arms around her older brother's waist, squeezing him tightly. Quin rested a hand on her shoulder, the fluttering touch of his magic wrapping around her to strip the worst of the mud and dirt away from her clothes. Even Ilo, standing with some of the other priestesses gave her the smallest smile of encouragement before Vinq turned to face the gathered villagers. The crowd parted to allow her to enter the circle where she was met by Mari, clad in a flowing gown, her face framed by curly strands of dark hair. There were a few murmurs from the crowd over the cracking of the bonfire, but Vinq tried not to listen to them.

"Did you bring an oak apple?" Mari asked, her voice barely a whisper.

Nodding, Vinq pulled the oak apple from her pocket and held it out. She was certain that Mari and the other priestesses could hear the loud clatter her heart was making in her chest. Mari didn't say anything about it being unprepared, she simply cupped it in her hands for a few moments until it was dried, then handed it to the next priestess to be turned into ink.

"Do you have your promise?" Mari asked next.

Vinq hesitated and glanced around at the people she'd grown up with. They had all come to see her move on to the next part of her life, even the youngest villagers who didn't know what the ceremony was about. Many gave smiled at her and a few even mouthed 'good luck' as she nodded, "Yes. I do."

A bowl and brush was handed to Mari and she smiled before drawing her hands up and over the two of them. A bubble formed around the two of them, locking out everything from the outside, except the light from the bonfire, "Then what is your promise, Vinq?"

Her throat was dry as Vinq held her hands out to Mari, who began to trace the appropriate symbols in the ink made from the oak apple she'd collected earlier. She cleared her throat, "I promise only to be myself. To love and protect the meadows, streams, trees, and animals that share the land with us."

Mari's eyes sparkled in the firelight as she drew the brush over Vinq's arms in broad strokes, then moved onto her cheeks, "You've always been a carer for the natural world around us. Is there more that you seek, beyond that?"

Vinq shook her head, feeling the ink start to dry on her skin, "No."

Nodding in acceptance, Mari set the brush and ink down and then took Vinq's hands, "Then I dub you the Lady of Spring. Protector of our natural world, bringer of seasons, greeter to the sun, rain, and snow. Do you accept your title?"

There had never been anyone in charge of nature to Vinq's memory. Most people held some useful position or job in the village. But as the silence drew on, Vinq could feel tears streaming down her face, "I do."

Mari kissed Vinq's cheek, allowing the temporary bubble to burst. The sounds of the fire cracking and children asking questions was suddenly back as Mari turned to the villagers with a smile, "Please welcome our Lady of Spring, Vinq!"

Cheers erupted from the villagers and she was hoisted on Hind's shoulder as the ink began to sink into her skin. She could already feel the connections she'd always had with the plants and animals growing stronger. The other priestesses sent up glowing sparks high above the tallest trees and the musicians of the village broke out their instruments to play.

Eventually Hind let her down so that he could dance and Vinq found herself watching everyone celebrate in the rainstorm. Mari tapped on her shoulder and held out a bouquet of wildflower blossoms to her, "Congratulations."

Vinq took the flowers, feeling her cheeks growing red, "Thank you."

"I'm happy you'll be doing something you like," Mari told her.

"I didn't think someone could be in charge of nature."

Mari smiled, "Well, not just anyone. You."

"What if I mess it up?" Vinq asked her,

trying to hide the concern in her voice.

"It's what you're meant to do. Look," Mari looked down at the bunch of wildflowers which were slowly opening their brightly colored petals as Vinq held them.

"But I'm not doing that."

"Aren't you? Flowers usually close at night. You know, I was nervous after my coming of age ceremony too."

"You couldn't have been. It was obvious you would be a priestess."

Mari shook her head, "I was worried I might not be good enough. Or that a mistake had been made."

Vinq took Mari's hands and smiled, "You're the best priestess. You know all the ancient hymns and spells and you're definitely the best dancer."

"Better than your sister?"

"Much better than my sister."

Pulling Vinq towards the bonfire, Mari asked, "Would you dance with me then?"

Vinq was speechless, she set the flowers down and nodded enthusiastically. They joined the revolving line of dancers which was moving around the bonfire, Mari far more sure on her feet than Vinq. But the anxiety of earlier in the day was melting away as the rain dripped down the back of her neck, replaced with laughter. It was the last night before she would take on the challenge of safeguarding the land, and she was going to enjoy it.

Vinq combed her hand through a stand of wildflowers as she waited for the sun to rise. The petals carefully opened, stretching out skyward. Bees and butterflies would soon be out to pollinate the meadow and the first of the village's crops. Field mice scurried back home to their holes after their nocturnal explorations and the hawks tried to spot them before they could make it to safety.

She didn't feel like she needed to hide in the meadow anymore. Her siblings and the rest of the village knew exactly where she was. There was never a shortage of work to be done in the valley. New fungi had been found by some of the children behind one of the old sheds, and one of the farmers was worried about the ducks rooting up his seedlings while they hunted for worms. Wrangling animals and plants and people to live harmoniously was more difficult than Vinq could have ever imagined. But the work was worth standing on the hill at sunrise and wondering what the new day would bring.

ABOUT THE AUTHOR

Cay Fletcher is a Queer author with a passion for fantasy and science fiction. Crafting rich landscapes and memorable characters in new and exciting worlds.

Living in the Portland metro area, Cay spends her free time in the garden, cooking, or making a mess, aka crafting. She spent over fifteen years volunteering at fan conventions across the US, and still occasionally assists her home convention in Portland by moderating guest panels. As a writer, Cay strives to create relatable queer characters, giving them the titles of hero and protagonist.

She lives with her wife Sam, their roommate and tuxedo cat Satsuki.

You can connect with Cay on social media or Goodreads.

www.cayfletcher.com

@cayfletcher

NEWSLETTER

Want to be the first to get the news?

Stay up to date with new releases by subscribing to my newsletter.

www.cayfletcher.com/newsletter

www.ingramcontent.com/pod-product-compliance
Lightning Source LLC
Chambersburg PA
CBHW032253070726
47590CB00016B/2647